T0028640

Requiem for a Manual Typewriter

Jonas Mekas

REQUIEM
FOR A
MANUAL
TYPEWRITER

Jonas Mekas with Sunshine, New York, 1974
Photo: Hollis Melton

Here is a huge roll of computer paper I found under my table. It was intended for some other purpose. Actually, it was intended for no purpose. There was a thick layer of dust on it. It was a roll of paper condemned to a miserable waste, I think. This evening I looked at it— I saw it, really, by accident, right there on the floor, as I was emptying my paper basket. Yes, I saw this roll of paper, and I remembered I put it there a few years ago, and I remember, this woman from Australia was here that evening, that day, Mrs. Hopkinson, now I remember, Mrs. Hopkinson was her name, she saw me placing it under the table, and she was looking at it, and I said, ah, what a waste, all this computer technology is such a waste of paper, I think I will write a novel on it, some day, it's such a nice roll of paper.

So now I picked it up, from under the table, from the floor. I wiped off the dust from it. I had some problems putting it into my Olympia De Luxe typewriter, but I did it. And here I am: I am on the first page of my novel. How does one begin a novel? Especially a novel of some importance?

It's as simple as this:

Here I am. I am nowhere. My life has come to a miserable crossroads. Red light, green light. Or crash.

Yes, I am absolutely nowhere and I am considering and reconsidering everything, and everything is without any end, any answers, and as blank and endless as this roll of paper, and, believe me, it's a very heavy big roll of paper. That's my life right now.

Dear Rousseau. Dear Augustine. Dear Kathy Acker. Dear Lynne Tillman. Dear Richard Foreman: This is my life.

Sebastian is playing Sonata No. 4 by Handel, it's very sweet. What this has to do with my novel? Absolutely nothing. But I am writing this down because I've decided to write a novel that is absolutely about nothing. I have absolutely no idea how long it will be, or whether I'll have enough patience or time or guts to finish it—that is, if a novel about nothing can or should be finished. But I have decided, I decided that the finishing line will be when I reach the end of this roll of computer paper. My only fear is that due to my total ignorance of computers, I cannot judge, I have no idea at all how many "typewriter" pages this roll of paper contains. I may be typing and typing and typing with no end until the year 2000, this being, right now, this very minute, only March 25th of 1997.

Ah, but what an unpredictable disaster! I have just discovered that the top part of this huge ecstatic roll of paper is sitting heavily on my table and there is no mechanism to really roll it up. It's just too heavy. So I have to make some decisions what to do about it. And it's a distraction from my efforts to keep readers' attention on this page. Yes, that's the main thing. I have read this in all books. A good writer has to keep the reader interested in what he/she reads. Ah, what a horrible thing. My computer paper just broke to pieces. It still holds, but there is a horrible gap in it. I hope it will hold, because it would be a pity to have this novel end right here because the whole point of this novel was that it's in one piece! Of course, every novel has to give the impression that it's in one piece. But I wanted it also to be on one piece of paper. But now I see that only one inch of it is still holding.

And ah, I see another gap coming. I hope it's not worse than the first one. I hope it will hold my novel together for a longer while although it looks pretty bad. This is something for the literary critics, actually, not me. These gaps are very natural, accidental, they have nothing to do with the intended plot or subject or whatever.

I have to interrupt, excuse me. I have to try to roll up this paper that is coming out of my typewriter, I have to try to roll it up somehow, because it's breaking up—the paper and the novel are so intertwined.

10

Ah, yes, forgive me the interruption. I think I have figured out how to protect this paper, how to roll it up so that my novel could continue, even if the line I am typing runs into the previous line. But isn't that how all life goes, or happens, or is? It's very very, it's almost three times very amazing how little insignificant accidents like typewriter lines slipping into each other because of the heavy roll of paper, how it effects what you write, it's amazing what it does, how it is, and what it means, if one looks at it very very sharply? Amazing. Have you ever thought about it, how amazing, really amazing life is? I never really thought about it that way but I am thinking about it that way now ...

But my novel is under attack! I see this horrible break. I had to roll up the paper, to protect it from breaking up completely. Now, my dear reader, what lessons can we take from this? Telling the truth, a good novel, a good story has to always, all the time, according to Ken Jacobs, has to keep breaking up, otherwise it's boring. So maybe it's good that my paper is breaking up, this gives me time or chance to consider other things. I do not mean thinking. Because I hate thinking. I am not a thinking person. Usually people don't believe me when I tell them that. But it's true. Yes, I am not a thinking person. Not really, but whatever is meant by "really." I just thought, which is amazing for a man who is never thinking, I just had a thought: could it be possible that nobody ever and ever and ever thinks? That all of that phony thing that we call thinking is only a reflection, an automatic, mechanical reaction, like in kung fu? Ah?

But this is late at night as I am typing all this nonsense, determined to fill this whole roll of paper with my typing.

This is later. Much later. August 5th, I think. Have you ever tried to write a novel? What a stupid question. Have you ever tried to write a novel when you have no time to write? When you are so consumed by daily bureaucratic

activities that you don't even want to think about
writing? That's where I am now. But I made a mistake.
I sat down by my table, and I saw the typewriter,
and I HAD TO WRITE. As soon as I see a typewriter,
I have to write. It sounds, I know, it sounds totally crazy,
but that has been my life's story. Paper and typewriter.
I see paper and I immediately think about writing
on it, I see typewriter, and I go nuts. Writing has nothing
much to do with anything else. It's all paper and
typewriter. Yes, Monsieur Derrida. Here it is, maybe
I am the ultimate deconstructivist, even if I don't look
so. Nothing really means anything. Words, just words.
Or, more correctly, letters. You just sit down and type.
That's all it takes. Letter after letter, word after word.
It could be one word, or another—makes not much
difference. It's just typing. Literature, my friends,
has nothing to do with the real world, out there, if there
is such a thing, as real world.
     All there is, is typing. Words, typing words.
     And they are all there, in the dictionary.
And alphabetically arranged, if you like bureaucracy.
Dictionaries are bureaucratic arrangements of words,
for the students and professors. Not for me. Maybe
for Jackson Mac Low. I used to watch Jackson, at Bob
Stock's apartment, standing there in front of this huge
dictionary which was placed on a special pult (lectern)
kind of table or desk, which Robert had placed in
the center of his room, it looked a little bit like an altar,
very very sacred, the way Robert had placed it there,
somewhere around 10th Avenue and 44th Street,
somewhere there, and there was Jackson Mac Low,
and Bob, talking about words, and I was amazed how
much they knew about the dictionary and the origins
of each word and their histories, I am still amazed about
it all even today—and of course that's why I consider
Jackson Mac Low the greatest English-language poet
today no matter who thinks what. Boy, now I'll have
enemies, I shouldn't have written this. But this is not

12

a novelistic content. I suppose to write about human emotions, feelings, thoughts, and conflicts of all kinds, but I keep straying away, which is not very promising for me, as a budding novelist. I think I really have to find my subject, my story, otherwise I think I am a goner, if there is such a word. I mean, if the word goner is accepted in serious literature because, I tell you, I want to be taken seriously.

NO NO NO. This is getting too pedantic, too serious. I have to abandon this line of writing if I really want to succeed as a novelist. I really want to succeed. I want to prove to Richard, Richard Foreman, if nothing else, that I also can write a novel, in parts or in no parts. A very different novel. Look: Richard has many tiny little stories, many pieces in his novel. It resembles more 1001 *Arabian Nights* than a novel. So, he says, it's a novel. So why not me? At least I can say that I am more in a Tolstoyan tradition: I have no 1001 stories: I have only one Big Story to tell, and I am trying to tell it. I have forgotten it, but I am trying to remember it, the story, I mean, the real story. I know I'll remember it as I am typing. Yes, typing. Yes, that's what this is all about. Typing. Typing is a very serious thing. It produces words, and words produce sentences, and sentences want to be connected so you begin to think how to connect them, it's a kind of engineering.

But now I am having a serious new problem, I am having some problems with the keys of my Olympia De Luxe typewriter. Wait, now it seems OK, yes, and maybe the problem was not Olympia's at all but the fact that I think I have drunk a full bottle of wine, while I was typing. I am quitting anyway, both wine and typing, for tonight.

This is much later. Many days, many weeks, months, actually. And this is very very late at night and I am so tired from all my bureaucratic daily activities, I can barely keep my eyes open. But my writer's ambition tells me I should continue. I should never give up. In addition, I believe that the best time to write anything, maybe not anything but a novel, is very late at night when one is completely tired. It's then that nothing can interfere with the true void, or writing, or anything, really.

But, my God, here is a real disaster: something is terribly wrong with my typewriter ribbon. I bought it from sheer pity, I wanted to help this stationary guy who had just opened, or, more correctly, reopened his store—he was about to go out of business—but this ribbon is so short, God, it's so short. I have to keep switching it from right to left every five minutes, it's so short. Which also means that my Olympia De Luxe is failing. The switching should be all automatic. But my Olympia has its own character. I cannot tell it what to do.

Anyway, here I am writing again. Writing! I am typing again. Ah, what a good feeling, just to type. I don't understand, why writers always want to write ABOUT SOMETHING when you can just type and type and type. The writers. They spend so many sleepless nights and they walk around worrying and they drink themselves to death trying to figure out what to write about, when, in truth, I see it now very clearly, there is no need for any subject at all! If you are a writer, then you just write, like me right now. You just write, or, if you want, you just type. Do you really want to be a writer, you there? So just sit down and write! Who was it who said it? I think it was Sinclair Lewis, he wrote *No Pasaran*, or was it Upton Sinclair, he wrote *The Jungle*, I always confuse those two because of that word, Sinclair. Anyway, I read them both as a little kid, maybe I was ten, and he said to these dopey literature students at this university, somewhere in America, where he was invited to speak to them about how to become a writer ... "So you want to be writers? So sit down and write!" And that was it. That's how the legend goes—

he walked out after saying that. Bless him. Because
I see nothing wiser than that. The ecstasy of just writing!
Pure writing, pure singing, it's all the same. You just
sing. Or you just write. Or, forgive me, you just film.
You don't make films, you just film. Why make films when
you can just film? Ah, what ecstasy just to do something!
Anything, absolutely anything! That's what I call
celebration of life! I am just that kind of person … Mad?
No. I think I am one of the most normal people around.
Actually, to tell you the truth, I think that most of
the people around me are pretty abnormal. In many ways.
Physically, mentally, sexually, extraterrestrially, etc.
Name any of it. I don't understand any of them. There
are times, actually, it was this afternoon, I was walking
down the Mulberry street and thinking that I really
don't know anything about the real world and real people.
Real? What the hell is real? Every moment of my life
I face people, situations that baffle me.

Sorry, but my typing was interrupted at this
point by a little argument with Sebastian who had just
interrupted his violin practice to complain about the
flies. There are more and more of them coming through
the open windows. So I said, tomorrow you have this
project: you go to Chinatown and buy some fly paper—
you know, those sticky things that you hang on the
ceiling and as time goes, it becomes, at least that is my
experience, everybody points at this thing, full of flies,
thousands of flies stuck on it, and they say: Is this some
kind of work of art? And some of them mean it seriously.

Sorry for this digression.

This really disrupted the flow of my typing.
I wanted to say "thinking," but I caught myself.
Really, it's "typing." I was also distracted by this stupid
typewriter ribbon. So, in order to straighten myself
out, I went to the fridge and poured myself a glass
of Portuguese wine, and emptied half of the glass in one
gulp, so now I am in a normal typing form. Or at least
I was. Because now Oona just came home and started

15

some kind of sister/brother argument about Sebastian
playing violin too loud, or something like that—one
of those very essential brother/sister situations that are
totally about nothing—ah, nothing, this being the basic,
essential theme of this whole novel, which should
be actually called, a NOVEL ABOUT NOTHING. But
I ain't going to name it that way, the idea has been
overused. The writing world is so unbelievably well read
and smart that they get ahead of you. After all, with
all those millions of books published every year, I think
that practically absolutely everything has been already
written. Sebastian is practicing his violin right next
to my right ear with the intention, so says Oona, to drive
me crazy. But I am very very sane, or at least still sane,
only my typing got all mixed up. Ah, all these distrac-
tions. But maybe that is a blessing, as Stan would say.
You know, Stan calls everything a Blessing, that's Stan.
I wonder what Stan is doing, how is he? I am always
so busy, I neglect my friends, I don't call them, I almost
avoid some of them. I don't know how I got caught
in all this worldly business, how I have lost grip on time.
I have time for nothing except this typing. Typing,
without knowing why I am typing. One supposes to
know what one is doing. But I have no idea at all, no idea
of any kind. Actually, I hate ideas. I am even suspicious
of people who have ideas. Lately I've developed this
theory, that people who have ideas are really very
dangerous. Yes, ideas are identical with PLANNING.
I have an Idea … I have a Plan … That's what they say.
A Plan. Panama Canal. My feeling is that behind every
plan, behind every idea there is a gun, or a tank, or
an atom bomb. Or at least a pistol. Even if it's an old
Browning. Bad enough. And I don't like any of it.
What I like is the sound of rain on cabbage heads. Ah,
what a sound! No movie, no poem has given me a greater
pleasure ever. Call me a moron. Anti-culture. I don't
care. But the sound of rain on cabbage heads, in a cabbage
field--ah, if you have never experienced it, been with it,

no use telling it to you, you'll never understand it. Because it's indescribable. That sonority. That quality of sound. Richness. Fullness. What can I say.

Another paper break…
Just when I was about to begin to tell my life story. All the ups and downs of my life. Ecstasies and miseries. But now I am totally distracted. I have to begin from the beginning. I am trying to concentrate. Not the kind of concentration when you see people's foreheads getting all very tense, no. I have in mind the concentration that I have seen when Ken, Ken Kelman, concentrates on his pills, I mean his vitamin pills of which he carries this little box full, these dozens and dozens of pills of all kinds of shapes and colors and sizes—but I have no interest in pills or health, I think health is a fad.

But I have this ribbon that is so short, so miserably short that I have to keep stopping every five minutes, to rewind it—and now Howard Stern is yapping on TV, his voice is distracting me. Now, just think, what all of this has to do with the essence of a good modern novel? I think I am doing pretty well so far, no? Especially, with all these breaks. Pretty deep stuff, open to a lot of post-graduate papers. Good luck, my young friends.

I know how Ken, I mean Ken Jacobs, likes breakings of every possible kind in his films, but I really hate these breakings in my computer paper roll, I hope this was the last one. Breaking, breaking. I keep saying it to myself. What's the meaning, cosmic, essential, elemental meaning of Breaking? It's a kind of entertainment tactic, gimmick, no? Short patience. For people who are so tense that they need a break every ten minutes. Great! Great! Let's have a break. Or let's break it down. Break it up! Theories of destruction. Destruction art. Broken hearts.

I promise you, I'll finish this novel even if I have to glue these pages with scotch tape. Anyone else would just quit. That's what a normal person would do.

But you see I am far from normal. I am taking this as a
challenge. Yes, like climbing Mt. Fuji or something like
that. I said Mt. Fuji because I am looking at a Mt. Rainier
postcard that somebody—who?—I forgot, what a shame—
somebody gave it to me the other day—it looks just like
Mt. Fuji right here, on my table—so it's like climbing
Mt. Fuji, to the very tip of it, yes, I hope I'll make it.

Sorry, I just had to switch my ribbon to go to the left.
Not to the political left, but simply left, no Marx or
Engels here, especially no Lenin who said "have no pity
for the Ukrainian farmers," and "get the Lithuanians,"
and mind, I am quoting this from memory because it got
burned into my memory, that's how much I love Lenin,
tovarish Lenin. So—forget the political left, even if
Ken—maybe?—is with it. Suddenly I thought: how many
Kens do I know? The two I have already mentioned,
should never be confused, they are very very very
different, Ken Jacobs and Ken Kelman. Yeah, the concentration with which Ken Kelman approaches, studies
his pills: it's kind of Zen, I think, it's like reaching the
very top of Mt. Fuji—I imagine—that kind of concentration, or meditation I think, yes, that's Kelman looking
at his pills. Yes, how many Kens do I know? Kenneth
(not Ken!) Anger. Kenneth Frampton. Who else, Ken
Rubin, Barbara's brother, she called him Kenny. And yes,
Kenneth, what's his last name, he wrote this book
on Ezra Pound. And Kenneth Patchen, I have his novel
there on the shelf.
          But now it's after midnight and I have to make
a pause in my novel. As I sleep, you are welcome to
meditate on the essence and meaning of "pause." Actually,
there is no pause, in a "real" novel. But—and here
is a surprise—for the illumined mind—: this, actually,
is a REAL novel. So you understand, when I say "pause"
or "real" or etc. it's all part of it—it's all calculated,
this is all a calculated, very calculated writing, this is a
calculated improvisation, one that is supported by my

whole life, if I may say so. Thus, in reality, if you really
want to know the truth, there is no improvisation here
at all: it's all the way it should be, it's all predetermined,
down to the last letter or finer slip. There are absolutely
no accidents in this whole universe, I have to tell you
that, my dear reader, not even this little comma, but the
real miracle of life, or literature, which is absolutely
the same, is that I found this roll of dust covered computer
paper under my table, it's this paper that has it all in it,
and I am only a typist, not much else, because, as I have
already told you earlier, I never think, I just do things,
or type things, or say things, or whatever, I react.
All my talk, whatever I say, is only responsive, reactive
jiu-jitsu —I have no thoughts or ideas of my own, sorry
for the commas, but I think commas were better, in this
case, than periods—I had intended periods, but my
fingers prefer commas, which contains another deep
meaning, the difference between the fingers and the
mind, what the finger thinks and what the brain thinks,
and both are of the same material, they both think,
even if the Stuyvesant School textbooks don't tell that.
I have a big revelation here for you: the fingers and
the brain have the same thinking ability!

Do you think I am joking? No, not at all.
Now I really feel sleepy. I have to go to bed. I will finish
my glass of wine and I'll go to bed. Sorry I have to
interrupt my novel. I am especially sorry about the wine.
White wine. Because in America today everybody
suppose to drink RED wine, because it's so good for
your health! But ah, can you imagine, what they will
write, when they will discover what the WHITE wine
does?

Yes, but this is not serious. This was a joke.
I want to be serious even if seriousness is not the most
popular thing today in the world. Seriousness. How
about that, seriousness as a subject of a novel? What is,
really, seriousness? Telling the truth, I have never
thought about it seriously ... Seriously ... Seriosity as

the Essential? To be Serious, to touch the Essence?
The desire of the Essence, of the Deepest, of the Most
Essential—Deepest Self? Or just simply Self? God?
Universe? All the Ancestors? Connectedness to All the
Ancestors? Yes, that's what I want this novel to be about.
But I cannot do it unless I am serious about it. Yes.
I don't think that anything of substance can be done in
this world—or on this piece of paper, for that matter—
if one is not serious. Like fake bread, or any fake thing.
It's all fake. Fake bread is not serious. Fakedness is not
serious. Ersatz is not seriousness. Perversion of seriousness is ersatz. This paper, so far, is just paper, that
means, it's serious.

Ah, my feet feel cold. I just took off my socks,
I am barefooted now. Just think for a moment, what
"barefooted" means in modern terms? The word "bare,"
for instance. I have to warn you, however, that this
has nothing to do with the Deconstruction, Derrida, etc.
This is just plain, bare talk. I'll talk about Derrida with
Richard, when I see him next. Me, I am just a plain folk.
Dum. Great to be dum, today. To be dum—I wish I could
be really and totally dum—to be dum is to be in bliss,
"to develop a mind that rests on nothing whatsoever," that
was a sign I had written and scotch-taped on the wall,
right in front of my working table, in 1955. It's still
my guiding light, I am still moving towards it. This novel,
of course, is all part of it, of this process to develop
a mind that rests on nothing. To be outside of our stupid
civilization. George managed to be so, I mean, outside,
but who else? Not easy, not easy, my dear readers.

But ah, this is horrible, really horrible.
Ah, how imperfect, how imperfect the computer paper
rolls are … It broke again … Horrible, horrible. I have
lost my thought, whatever there was left of it. Now it's
all gone.

You have to admit: I am an idealist. Or at least
I was. I thought I will make a bridge between the manual
old-fashioned typewriter, more precisely, my Olympia

De Luxe, and the modern, contemporary computer technology, via this roll of computer paper. But I have to admit I am failing miserably. Will the two ever meet? No, no hope. I see no hope for it. So this is, in a way, a miserere, or, OK, a requiem for the old days' typewriter, a typewriter with a real sheet of paper in it, where you feel your fingers touching the keys and you feel the paper, and the roller, line by line, as you roll—ah, what an ecstasy!

You must have already noticed that I have completely given up on the computer paper roll. Which is a pity. I had no choice, it just kept breaking up. And the quality of paper was terrible. Paper was thin, pale, sickly. No substance of any kind. Not like real paper. I wonder what has happened to the production of paper. There is no more decent paper. It's all Xerox paper. How can you write a novel on Xerox paper? It was I guess my carnal mistake to begin this novel on computer paper. I should have known better. The essence of computer is not novelistic. It's something else. It's a mystery to me what it is. To me, to really want to write is to see REAL capital letters, REAL paper. That's why I am typing now. On a real piece of paper I found on a dusty pile of scribbles. It was, or rather still is blank. Now, a horrible thought. Since this is the only sheet I have for today, I have to be very condensed, I have to say something really great that would propel my novel forwards and would engage you so totally that you would anxiously wait, like the Dostoyevsky readers in St. Petersburg one hundred years, actually more, ago, for his feuilletons... for the new issue of *St. Petersburg Gazette* yes, please wait, I will now tell you the biggest secret of my life that set me on this disastrous road—just turn to the next page—tomorrow—when I get more paper—

This is another day.
I went to Staples and bought for myself a ream of nice plain white paper. Just to be sure I don't run out of paper.

So now— GLORY GLORY ALLELUJAH! I am typing on a real sheet of paper. Just paper. So all my worries have been eliminated now. Worry? Me?

I am worrying more about Allen, I just spoke with him, and he has a liver cancer and he said, in a quiet, weak, but to my assessment, jolly voice, that he has only three months to live, and we conversed about that, and laughed, and yes, it is amazing, pretty amazing, that here it is, he is going to die in three months, but we are joking and laughing and paying no attention to it all. Doesn't this sound a little bit strange to some of you? I bet it does. But Allen was really OK. I have to admit that I was a little bit confused. Here he is, almost dying, even if not yet, but dying slowly, and here is me. For at least a fraction of a second I was lost. Should I console him? Say I am sad about it? Etc. etc. Luckily, I forgot it all and I slipped back into my old regular self and we had just a regular conversation. A happy conversation.

Ah, I have no idea what all this is all about. It's certainly not about death. I was talking to Allen, and we both were OK, but there was, nevertheless, a note, some kind of note, in the back of my mind, that yes, this may be our last conversation.

I put down the receiver and Hollis passed by and I said, that was Allen and he is dying.

Julius is leaving next Tuesday. Friday—Sophie's party for Julius. My wine glass is empty. Mount Rainier postcard on my table in front of me is incredibly beautiful. Now put all these little facts together, make a collage.

No, no, no. I have, I must make this novel much more personal. Not as personal as Anäis Nin's Diaries, but something approaching closely to it. Yes, she called me a communist. I really wonder what her idea of a communist was... But she wrote this letter, telling, or accusing, now it's so far back, I don't really remember— but I can check it, I still have her letter—have it stacked somewhere because I never throw anything away, that is another of my vices or rather habits which I do not wish for anybody and you would realize why, if you'd see my apartment and know all the problems that I have now, since we have decided to sell our apartment, my problems deciding how many and what size boxes I have to order, for packing, with Soho now full of boutiques and fashion and all the paper box places gone, gone, gone—

Now, now. This is a real disaster, my friends. I mean, Richard, Lynne, Kathy, all my writing friends, Vyt, yes, Vyt, because where would I be without Vyt. The disaster I am talking about is this; I have, by accident, mixed up all the pages of my novel. Unintentionally. Just by pure chaos of my existence. I have to reveal to you now my probably biggest weakness: my inability to organize myself, that is, to somehow organize my incredible chaos. Total lack of organizational skills, so to say. All my papers, all my pages just float around me. Thomas Wolfe at least dropped his pages under the table, I read it somewhere, in a huge pile, so there was a natural order of a pile where the last sheet on top is always the last sheet on top. But in my case, they all float all around the table, and when I lose something, and that happens ten times a day, I just take all the pages from one pile and put them on top of another pile and then still on another as I desperately search for a missing letter or whatever it happened to be. You get the idea.

Horrible, horrible, I tell you. And all that wasted time looking for something lost. That's the story, another story of my life, looking for things lost. But as I am typing now, all of this, in my typing ecstasy, I just had a genius thought, and that is, there is a possibility that no, I am never ever ever losing anything. The truth is that I am only misplacing it all, putting it in some other place. But yes, yes, I am going to find it all again, I will find it all again or I will simply blunder upon it, bump into it all again, someday ... my whole past ... No, no, no, nothing is ever lost, that is the main idea I think of this novel, if anyone needs one. And the fact that I have mixed up the pages changes nothing essentially. Everything, all life is only a big messy collage and you can start it at any point and it would still come out the same, absolutely the same, my friends. Do I, by saying this, deny the act of will? Our divine nature? Please do not ask me any of such questions because I know nothing about such matters. All I know is typing. I think with my fingers, that is, if I do any thinking at all.

Maybe I should stop right here. Because suddenly I noted something really horrible: I had started this page with a new PARAGRAPH. Imagine that? To begin to think and write in paragraphs? Horrible, horrible. Anyway, a thought that crossed my mind is, or rather was, since I am now a few minutes ahead or behind the time, the thought was/is/was that my novel has no sex, no sex at all, and therefore, who's going to read it! I don't think anyone reads these days anything that doesn't reek of sex. But tell me, dear friends, how can I get sex into this, I just can't, because that's an entirely different world, and, to tell you, or rather confess to you, I know absolutely nothing about it. Did I ever know anything about it? No. And I'll never know. A total mystery. Like all humanity, believe me or not, all life, all humanity to me is nothing but a mystery. I know nothing about it. I don't understand it, I don't know how to deal with it, I have no idea how I manage to go from one day to another, what I do, or why I do what I do, and why my life is still going, why doesn't it stop, like, say, for Emilia, she was only fifteen, we graduated together from the Primary School, and I am walking home one day, and I see her sitting in a carriage, on top of bags full of barley or something, and she looked so regular and aged, she looked like thirty. I had heard before, from the neighbors, that she was forced to marry this guy, this farmer. So here she was, she was sixteen, or maybe seventeen by that time, and we looked at each other and there was this huge world in between us, because I was still just a kid, and there was she, a married woman, part of the real life, REAL LIFE. What is it, what is it, why am I not part of the real life, how can I become a part of it, how? Of course, there is no answer, there is no answer, you can type as fast as you can and as long as you want, like Henry Miller, bless him, we visited with Arunas yesterday in Williamsburg and walked through all the streets, the Second, and the Third, and the Fifth, and them all, and I said to Arunas, you know Henry Miller lived here, and then we continued, searching for Ginkus Candy Store, but there was no longer Ginkus Candy Store there, there was some kind of travel agency, so I said let's have a beer, I was so depressed, remembering all the beers I had at Ginkus Candy Store—so we went to this Mexican place, and had Dos Equis, and there were all those Mexican sombreros hanging on the walls, and this guy was sleeping in the corner with a bottle of beer still in his hand, so the bartender came and gently took the glass away so it wouldn't fall on the floor, and we paid and walked out into the streets of Williamsburg, Brooklyn—

So where the hell is sex here. No no no, none of it, only bare, down-to-earth life here, and misery—but I need another glass of wine now. No, I didn't get sex into my novel at all by telling the story of Emilia, I got only huge sadness that is now floating around me, around my Olympia De Luxe and this table, and my head, summer sweat, a huge sadness, thinking about Emilia's unrealized life, sitting there on top of those bags of barley or whatever, at the age of fifteen, you don't know how often this image has come to me, to my memory, during all these years, this image of unrealized life, frozen at fifteen—I tremble, I almost cry by thinking about it, remembering that meeting on a hot summer road, dusty, hot—so where am I? No, I never know where I am. I don't think I ever knew. Is that a blessing or a curse,

not to have any plan, not to know or even care where you
are, not to know what to do, to permit life to take its
own course? A weakness? Am I weak? No willpower?
I have dismissed the willpower long ago, I threw it out
the window on Linden street, Brooklyn, many years ago.

Now, this is ten minutes later. Because Oona,
when I was typing the previous lines, Oona who was
skipping through the *New York Times,* this is, by
the way, August 4th 1997—she just said: Hmm, William
Burroughs died. Which caused me to stop, my fingers
stopped right there. What?—I said. I heard it on the
radio, she said, but it's also here in the *New York Times.*
I went to the table and looked at the paper, and there
it was. So, he's gone too. I still remember the excitement
when I saw the *Big Table* issue with the first install-
ment of *Naked Lunch* and I remember reading it
non-stop in one sitting and then grabbing the phone
to call Louis Brigante and Storm De Hirsch to tell them
the Big News: here was a writer, a new great writer, I said,
and we sat all night reading and rereading all excited.

But this again has nothing to do with anything.
I shouldn't fall into the trap of memories, sentimental
memories. So, go away, all that nonsense of the Sixties,
the first meetings, the first this and the first that.
I don't quite understand why George was so obsessed
with pinning down the firsts—Malevich did this first,
Duchamp did that first, Schwitters did this, or George
Brecht, or Yoko Ono or La Monte and etc. and etc.—
he always cared only about the first, who did what for
the first time, and he knew it all. And we stupids,
we sang all those folk songs in Lithuania, in our little
village, not knowing, not even thinking that there was
somebody first. We should have just closed our mouths,
our stupid loud mouths and gone to sleep or something,
instead of singing. No, we were not the first ones
to sing them, not the first ones at all, and we didn't
even care, you see, about art, because only in art is there
this One Time Thing and repeating it is a sin. So that

26

is where life and art part, I guess. But who cares. Let it all continue, flow by itself, let people argue, fight, write long serious essays in university quarterlies, which I can never read, but I think it's good that somebody takes time to write them, that only proves that some people take life and literature seriously, not like me. I don't take anything very seriously. I cannot admit to myself that there is something that should be taken seriously today.

I think I am beginning to lose my concentration. It's very very late. So I may quit. It's very tempting to write and write, or you could say, to type and type, until you collapse, and later, reading what you wrote, you see how your mind gradually collapses, falls to pieces, how nonsense takes over, like watching a drunk. I am not sure I am interested to go through such an experiment tonight, the more that it doesn't really work. I tried it once, to keep notes on one of my drinking and desperation evenings, when I thought nobody loved me, it was maybe in 1955. I decided to get drunk, because nobody loved me, so I went to one of the Eighth Avenue dingy places, and kept writing down every five or so minutes how I felt, as I kept drinking and going down the life's drain. I am not sure you'd be interested in all the little other details of that evening. But I read, later, or rather I tried to read all those drunk scribbles, and it was nothing, just an empty stupid indecipherable nothing. Like the dreams you try to write down, when still half asleep. Boy, it is great. But you read it in the morning, and it's nothing, pure nothing.

A sudden thought. Why am I writing all this nonsense down? I think I am doing it because Lynne Tillman is doing it and Kathy Acker is doing it and now even Richard Foreman is doing it. And yes, Ken Kelman is doing it, and believe it or not, even P. Adams Sitney wrote a novel once, I read it, I hope he hasn't burned it or something, because it was quite interesting, he wrote it when he was seventeen, or something like that. So why not me, and I am much older and smarter and know more about life. No matter what I write, it will contain more human eternal wisdom and knowledge than any of them, with the exception of Mme. Jeanne Calment, age 122, from Arles, who said she had met Van Gogh, when she was twelve or thirteen, she died today, I read it in the *New York Times*, and the obituary noted that she used "more than two pounds of chocolate every week and treated her skin with olive and rode a bicycle until she was 100 and only quit smoking five years ago." She liked to drink, too. Anyway, I think I have a lot of knowledge, if not wisdom. The only thing is, what's good knowledge and wisdom. You can't make any kasha out of it, as they used to say on Essex Street.

It's raining really badly out there, outside. It has been raining all evening. So this page is in a melancholy B-flat minor, or whatever key. My mind gets all woolly and whatever, what's the word, when it's raining.

This woman, last Saturday, Friday night, at Mars Bar, she was there, and I said, I don't know why, just from boredom I guess, I said, what do YOU do? Because she was with musicians. I thought she was a musician of some kind, I should have of course said, What do you play? But I made a mistake, small mistake, but a mistake. So she said, grumpily, "I write." We both returned to our beers. But an hour later, she attacked me. Ah, I forgot to tell you about my reaction to her when she said, "I write." You see, I made some face as when people tell me they are artists. I made a face, and said, hhhhmmm. I made a sound of hhhhmmm. So an hour later she told me that my reaction was "not supportive," and that I should be more supportive. So I said one of my tasks in life, what I do, is try to discourage people from writing or "being creative," and things like that. Do you really need encouragement to write? If you need, then please please do not write. In any case, I hope she will stop writing. Unless, of course, she is like me. In which case, she will continue. Like me, now. As long as I see a blank

28

piece of paper in my typewriter, my fingers get itchy, they have to type, and I sit and I type, and type, and without thinking, of course, I just type, aiming at nothing, hoping that my writing, my typing will be as empty, as much about nothing, as possible. And totally non-creative. I detest creativity. Creativity may be the No. 1 thing I detest most, in life and art. Cinema, especially in cinema. And food, yes, food. All those creative dishes, foods, especially by the New Age people, they make me sick just to look at them. So I go out and have a simple, old-fashioned hamburger, or a hot dog. There should be some way to punish people who do those creative things, they are enemies of normal human development, natural development. Now now now, what would Oscar Wilde say to such a statement, I suddenly thought. So what, dear Oscar, you can think what you want, I don't give a penny for your thoughts.

I just put another sheet of paper into my Olympia De Luxe. Raga music on radio, very nice, very nice. But I am being distracted. The ear, the ear. My right ear, that is. The radio is on the right. Now I am really distracted. I just had a gulp of white wine, I forgot what brand, what winery, that is, wine, hoping that it will restore my writing. But no. It stopped, suddenly, stopped dead. My novel, my dear friends, my dear readers, my novel has come to a dead stop, a crisis, like a Wall Street crisis, it fell flat on its face, in New York, in Singapore, Tokyo. No wine will help here. It's a flat flat evening. And I know why: it has been raining all day. And whenever it's raining, 100 percent humidity, my brain gets all muffled, everything stops, I even get depressed, those are the only times I get depressed … That is, usually I don't get depressed the way most people do or are. Which means, there is something very wrong with me. Maybe it's some kind of useless, impractical, I don't know what to call it, optimism, trust in life. Which, as you all well know, never works. Same as with my not understanding why people get angry. Actually,

I'll confess to you, this is confessional, one of the very rare confessional moments of my life—that may be another big problem of my life, not being confessional more often—I had this girlfriend, once, and when I told her that I don't understand anger—because my parents, I never witnessed them being angry—therefore, I said, whenever I see people being angry, I retreat, I just retreat, because I cannot deal with it, I don't understand how grown up people can get angry, lift their voices, produce strange qualities of voice sounds,—no, I don't understand any of it, so I become like a dog, I try to crawl under the table, like dogs do, and I lie down— you got the image? So this girl says, I don't believe you, but if that is really true then I'll do something one day, something that will make you really angry, because you have to experience anger. No, I said, I don't need it, why should I need to experience anger? Why do humans need it? Then, why not experience murder, robbery, and etc. and etc.? No, she said, but you need to experience anger. Why why? I said. You need it because otherwise you are not complete, she said. Why do I have to be complete? There is no end to completion, I said. Comple- tion is a fad. In any case, she disappeared and I never found out what she had planned to do to make me angry. That means, I will never achieve completeness. In situations, where others get angry, I become theatrical. I imitate angry people. The result, of course, is that then nobody takes me seriously.

But, bluntly, my dear friends, I do not want to be complete. What did life ever have anything to do with being "complete." It's all an invention to make humans miserable, this "complete" thing. I don't even know what it is. But it sounds very serious, very important, when you say that. Anyway, to be complete is to be dead, *n'est pas*? So leave me alone in my incompleteness. In chess, to complete is to check. Or to complete this novel. I have no intention to ever completing it, if you want to know the truth. That doesn't mean I intend to Proust you to death. Not at all. What it will be, I guess, I can only guess, because I am still pretty pepped up about this novel—what it will be, I guess, that I eventually will get tired of all this typing and all this ribbon changing every ten minutes or so, and that will be it, that will be the end, as chance, as casual and unpredictable and without any reason as anything else in this life of ours: never really "completed" but in truth always completed, because everything always IS and always will be complete, even if not completed—why does Louise Bourgeois' son always carry his suitcase with him through Praha, I was suddenly asked—and that is part of the completion —telephone always rings—I ignore it,—my brain is tired, complete in its tiredness—eleven thirty—a hard day—this has nothing to do with you, my dear readers, I am noting all this down only for myself—and the little pieces of paper with sex fantasies I found today in the office, covered with dust, while cleaning the place—and they are pretty good sex fantasies, and I got very excited when I found them and read them because I thought I could splice them into this novel, for your prurient, what's the word, interest. I haven't figured out yet which of my office workers has that kind of genius imagination to write them. I cannot imagine anyone I know in the office of Anthology who could have that much prurient talent. I may decide to insert these "found-sex-texts" into my novel, so do not skip any pages, please...

Now I am thinking. To tell you the truth, I stopped typing for a long minute and just sat, thinking: Have I really ever been angry? And I could not remember. I bet I have been. There must be degrees, variations of anger. Frustrations. Short temper. Is short temper anger? Little explosions.

Another interruption. I had to turn off some lights. It's midnight, actually, two minutes to midnight, to be precise. Lessons of Robbe-Grillet. Now I decided— this happened while I was turning off the lights—I mean, this thought came to me, I mean the thought that I

should try to think about the instances when I was really
angry, so now I am still thinking about it. But all I can
think is frustrations. Now, now, suddenly now something is coming into my memory. But I think it was the
anger on myself, not others. I remember, when I was
fifteen or sixteen, I told to my uncle, that I would like
to study theology and become a priest. And he said,
do you really mean that? And I suddenly understood that
I had said it only to please him, because my uncle was
a Protestant priest. That scene, that conversation, as we
were walking across a green summer field, has returned
back to me, in my memory, many many times, and every
time I have felt anger on myself for saying that to him
because I never really meant it, what I said. It was all
wrong. And every time I remember that conversation,
I get angry on myself for saying something I didn't really
mean. That was sixty years ago. But I still regret it.
How about that? Just a little one minute conversation
walking across a summer field with your uncle, and
saying something, and then it all comes back, for sixty
years, when so many things, births, deaths, disasters,
wars have been forgotten long long ago. How about that?
Essential things … Small things … ah, the essential
things that really matter … They seem at the time they
happen, so small, so insignificant … But while other
BIG things diminish, with time, these tiny things keep
growing … remain alive … ah, so real. So real even this
very moment I am writing this down …

   I have to apologize to you that this novel seems
to become more and more autobiographical. But so what.
The main thing is, it keeps me typing. It's not important
at all, you will read this or not. Because the main thing
is TYPING, my relationship with my Olympia De Luxe,
my fingers, these letters, this ribbon that is so short
that I have to keep switching it every five minutes or so—
that's all, that's all, my friends. It has nothing to do with
literature. But now I have to go to sleep. Tomorrow,
my dear Olympia De Luxe, I will be back with you.

I am back. How the time runs. This is February nineteenth. Nineteen ninety seven. And I am thinking. I do not know why, but it just came to me as I was sitting down. I never know what I am going to write before sitting down and rolling in another sheet of paper. But suddenly I began thinking. I am thinking about my TEN, TEN tortured years, 1939–1949. Occupations by foreign armies. Deportations, arrests of closest friends. Deportations of neighbors, deportations of school friends, same class, same bench. All the bad, horrible memories, dreams … graves … descriptions of tortures. Later, forced labor camps, factories, endless years in Displaced Persons camps … I don't know where to begin or stop enumerating it all. How can I be normal, like everybody else? Of course, I want to be normal, and I imagine I am, and I even have managed to give an impression, to pass for a normal person … But let's face it: that is impossible. That is IMPOSSIBLE. In reality, in truth, the horrible truth, the bottom essential reality is I am a nervous wreck. I could have a nervous breakdown right this minute but I am holding. I am holding it and I hope that I can hold it until my next reincarnation when it will all come tumbling down in thunder, like a thunder it will come, a thunderous nervous breakdown, my dear friends. Did you sleep well last night? Lisette asked me this morning. No, I said, I haven't. I think I haven't slept well since I was a child, I said.

Now this is a few days later.
I have come to a drastic decision which is: what I wrote till now, as a budding novelist, is all nonsense. What is my drastic decision, you want to know?:
      I decided to start it all from the beginning.
So here is the new beginning. I really believe that I am now on a better track, maybe even on the right track. Track, trek.
So here I begin.

I was walking. I was—
no, a slight change.
He was walking.
no, I go back to the first.
I was walking.
I was walking very slowly, very. You could say,
foot after foot, almost counting it all.
I was walking slowly, because it was about 105.
I was not sweating.
A green low branch brushed the edge of my hat.
Ah, I said, I connected with nature.
I turned around—slowly, of course, and went back—
two steps, really, to the tree and let a little branch full of
leaves slip through my fingers—
An old pantheist gesture, a regurgitation from my
pantheist Lithuanian past—
and then I continued my walk.
I had no purpose. I had not decided what I wanted to do.
I was just walking. I could not detect any thought in my
head. I was not thinking, as far as I can tell now,
as I am writing this down.
What is this "kissing and kissing again over and over
and I wake up" on radio.
Time: 12:32min. The voice says ... I just missed it.
I am not sure this new beginning is working. But let us
continue.

Yes, I am walking and not thinking. I am walking this
street. It's DeKalb, it says so up there. Of course I am in
Brooklyn so you have no idea where I am because nobody
knows Brooklyn. I keep saying that to all my friends
and then I look at them straight and say, have you read
that short story by Thomas Wolfe and they stare back
at me and of course they have never read it, but I read
everything so I read it, and I know a lot about Brooklyn.

Where am I going?
I still don't know.

34

I do not feel like eating. The oysters in this place I am passing are always warm. I like cold oysters.

When I eat oysters I need to feel like they have just come from deep cold mysterious ocean spaces, waters.

I think a lot about water. I seldom drink it, I am not like Benn who consumes maybe three liters or more every day. When I am thirsty I drink wine. But this is neither here nor there. I mention this only because I have a great attachment to the oceans via oysters. But I am a Capricorn, a goat, and I never go to the oceans, beaches, water and me are like white and black, and the few times when I tried to swim I felt that it attacks me, it wants to swallow me, there is something in deep oceans that threatens me, some superpower, origin of life, it wants to take it back. I don't know what but whenever I am, say, in a boat—and the most horrible experience was when I was in the middle of the Atlantic on FRANCE, a big big ship, big boat, you know what ship I am talking about, it was big—and suddenly I felt that the ocean was determinedly attacking me, Poseidon or some other demon of the primordial depths, as if I was invading it, it was pulling me down and I had to use all force and ingenuity, yes, ingenuity not to be pulled down. It was testing me, I felt, it was attacking, testing my very being, like saying hey, here you are, you little nothing, and I can swallow you any time like a worm that you are, so what are you going to do about it? What do you have to show for yourself, what will be left of you, you, ah? So try to be yourself, and see how much of yourself there is, you little worm...

And so it went. It was unbearable. For seven days I had this dialogue with the Atlantic Ocean, day and night, awake and asleep, it was laughing at me, testing me, playing with me, and I, I was a little nothing three thousand miles from New York and three thousand miles from Paris, determined not to give in, not to give in, insisting that I was far far superior, far far ahead to all those waters, the urschlam, the urH$_2$O, and I was part of a civilization that had left waters long ago, had left fishes and turtles and now was part of the twentieth century civilization! And the only thing that still binds us is the oysters, you dum big thing! And all this was going, as I said, on this other big dum thing, the big ship called FRANCE.

I decided to stop for a beer. Corner of DeKalb and what? Why don't they write names of streets even if the street is small like this one.

At the table just in front of me a Black guy with a little, maybe a year-old, kid on his lap. The kid is very active. The guy's newspaper drops to the floor. The guy tries to reach for it, cannot because of the kid in his lap, he can not bend low enough. A huge ugly perambulator next to them. Huge. I decide to be civil. Let me save the situation, I say. I pick up the newspaper, *Daily News*, and hand it to the guy. Then I see the stroller again and my blood begins to boil. I have to tell you, dear reader, that I have this immense hate of baby strollers. I tell you, if I wouldn't be so involved in what I am doing, I would start a campaign for elimination of perambulators.

"Why do you need this ugly stroller, why don't you just carry the kid, close to you," I say to the guy. Then I stand behind the stroller and I say, "Look, you are here, pushing him like this, and the kid is there, seeing only what's in front of him, the street, the mad crowd, the strangers. Why do you do that to your kid?" The guy says, "But he likes it, it's OK." No, I want to say, it's not OK. But I don't. Because I see that the guy doesn't get what I am trying to say. So I say, "Yes, of course, it's OK," and I go back to my table. But the kid now thinks I am his friend. Not because of what I said about strollers but because I spoke to his father. So he keeps looking at me and smiling, friendly kind of way. I order a beer.

No air conditioner here in this place. I like that. I don't
mind it. I hate air conditioners. I am not a green activist.
I just hate air conditioners. I like normal air. I like heat.
Yes, I like heat. If it's summer then it must be hot,
for me. I must sweat. To me that's one of summer's
pleasures, to sweat.
But let us not get distracted by the heat, the summer.
Let us go back to the story.
It's another day.
I am going, he said.
Very often, it's a very strange habit of mine, I refer to
myself in the third person.

He walked out into the cool early fall street.
All this nonsense talk, he thought.
He continued walking towards DeKalb Avenue. He had
nothing urgent to do and nobody he would have liked
to see. So he just walked, not even hoping anything interesting to happen.
It felt good to be alone.
His girlfriend had left him on Thursday, now she is in
Mexico. Good riddance, he thought. He hated to argue,
and she thrived on it. Yes, good riddance. He suddenly
felt very free with the whole world before him on the
plate. He felt so happy he began to whistle which he
hadn't done for ages. On the corner of DeKalb he
stopped at his favorite Irish bar. Some local guys were
engrossed in a soccer game between some minor teams.
Guinness?—the waitress knew him very well.
How did you know?—he said laughingly.
He sat at an empty table by the window and looked at the
Sunday Brooklyn street.

But now, my dear reader, this is a real disaster. Just when
I thought I was really getting into the story, a real story
that I know, my intuition was telling me that I was really
beginning to get you interested in it, by it I mean my
story, a real story, and in the very heart of Brooklyn—

suddenly I had to stop. And for the stupidest reasons.
I remembered my last night's dream, suddenly it popped
up in my memory. I never remember my dreams, some-
times I even think that most of the nights I do not dream
at all, I just sleep, I become a huge emptiness, lying
there, totally empty. But this morning I was very sure
that I had a dream, I dreamt—but no memory trick,
no trying to remember helped me to retrieve it, pff.
It was gone. Gone like a dream, what a true expression.
Gone like a dream. But now, at the most improper time,
it just popped up in my head, just pop and there it was.
My fingers stopped froze in the air just before touching
the letter P.
How proper.

It was a very simple dream. I dreamt I was writing a
novel. But strangely, I wasn't writing it with my Olympia
De Luxe, I was writing it with a pen! And not with
those new stupid commercial pens, no: I was writing
with a real old-fashioned pen, do you know what I mean?
        A pen, can you imagine a pen? Not a pencil,
not a Magic Marker, please please please: it was a pen
that I dipped into the inkwell and I wrote, I wrote in my
dream, I dipped and I wrote and wrote. And as I wrote
I heard a tiny tiny sound, a scratch as it touched the
paper, as I dragged it softly over a sheet of blank white
paper, like I used to do when I was in the primary
school. Yes, I moved my hand along the page, and the tip
of the pen made the shapes of letters and wrote words
leaving beautiful traces of black ink, as the pressure
of my fingers split the tip gently as I occasionally dipped
it into the square glass jar of black ink and continued
writing. It's made of soft metal, the tip that's inserted
at the end of my wooden chopstick-like piece— exactly,
you can imagine, like the scribes of old times did,
and I have tried it myself, with a stork, a strong firm
stork feather—it's soft, it bends, so you have to be gentle
with it. All night, I dipped it into the inkwell, in my

dream, and I wrote and I wrote—all night I wrote. I wrote my novel, of course. In total silence of the night, late. No cars, no radios, no tv, no planes, because I was fifteen and I was in my village in Lithuania and there was nothing but silence and in that silence I could hear my ink pen, the gentle sweet sound of my pen as I was writing my novel. Then I stopped. My hand stopped moving. The sound of the pen stopped. I had finished writing the novel.

Now I looked at my finger, frozen on the letter P. And I tried to remember how I ended it, my novel, how I ended it, in my dream. But it was all gone, gone like a dream.

FILMOGRAPHY

FILM SELECTION FROM 1961 TO 2019

Guns of the Trees
1961, 87 minutes, b&w

Film Magazine of the Arts
1963, 17 minutes, b&w, color

The Brig
1964, 68 minutes, b&w

Award Presentation to Andy Warhol
1964, 12 minutes, b&w

Report from Millbrook
1966, 12 minutes, color

Hare Krishna
1966, 4 minutes, color

Notes on the Circus
1966, 12 minutes, color

Cassis
1966, 5 minutes, color

The Italian Notebook
1967, 15 minutes, color

Time and Fortune Vietnam Newsreel
1969, 4 minutes, color

Walden

1969, 176 minutes, color

Reminiscences of a Journey to Lithuania

1972, 82 minutes, color

Lost Lost Lost

1976, 174 minutes, b&w, color

In Between: 1964–68

1978, 52 minutes, b&w, color

Notes for Jerome

1978, 45 minutes, color

Paradise Not Yet Lost, or Oona's Third Year

1979, 97 minutes, color

Street Songs

1983, 11 minutes, b&w

cup/saucer/two dancers/radio

1983, 23 minutes, color

Erick Hawkins: Excerpts from "Here and Now with Watchers"/ Lucia Dlugoszewski Performs

1983, 6 minutes, b&w

He Stands in a Desert Counting the Seconds of His Life

1985, 149 minutes, color

Scenes from the Life of Andy Warhol: Friendships & Intersections

1990, 35 minutes, color

Carl G. Jung or Lapis Philosophorum

1991, 29 minutes, color

Zefiro Torna or Scenes from the Life of George Maciunas

1992, 37 minutes, b&w, color

On My Way
to Fujiyama I met...
1995, 25 minutes, color

Happy Birthday
to John
1995, 24 minutes, color

Memories
of Frankenstein
1996, 95 minutes, color

Birth of a Nation
1996, 81 minutes, color

Song of Avignon
2000, 9 minutes, color

Autobiography
of a Man Who
Carried his Memory
in his Eyes
2000, 53 minutes, color

As I Was Moving Ahead
Occasionally
I Saw Brief Glimpses
of Beauty
2000, 283 minutes, color

FILMOGRAPHY

Ein Märchen aus alten Zeiten
2001, 6 minutes, color

Mysteries
2002, 34 minutes, b&w

Williamsburg, Brooklyn
2002, 15 minutes, b&w, color

Travel Songs
2003, 28 minutes, color

A Letter from Greenpoint
2004, 78 minutes, color

Notes on an American Film Director at Work: Martin Scorsese
2005, 80 minutes, color

First Forty
2006, 193 minutes, b&w, color

Lithuania and the Collapse of the USSR
2008, 289 minutes, color

FILMOGRAPHY

Correspondences: Jonas Mekas – J.L. Guerín

2011, 100 minutes, b&w, color

Sleepless Nights Stories

2011, 114 minutes, color

Reminiszenzen aus Deutschland

2012, 25 minutes, color

Out-Takes from the Life of a Happy Man

2012, 68 minutes, color

Requiem

2019, 84 minutes, b&w, color

GRAPHIC DESIGN:
Hannes Drißner, Spector Books

IMAGE CORRECTION:
Scancolor Reprostudio GmbH

PROOFREADING:
Victoria Nebolsin
Sophia Holland

PRINTING AND BINDING:
Gutenberg Beuys Feindruckerei GmbH

ACKNOWLEDGEMENTS:
Sebastian Mekas and the Jonas Mekas Estate,
Hollis Melton, Christoph Gnädig

FILMOGRAPHY:
from 1960 to 1991 selection by Jonas Mekas,
from 1992 to 2019 selection by Christoph Gnädig

COPYRIGHTS:
© 2022, text: Jonas Mekas; photo: Hollis Melton;
Spector Books

Published by Spector Books, Leipzig
www.spectorbooks.com

DISTRIBUTION:

GERMANY, AUSTRIA:
GVA, Gemeinsame Verlagsauslieferung Göttingen
GmbH & Co. KG, www.gva-verlage.de

SWITZERLAND:
AVA Verlagsauslieferung AG, www.ava.ch

FRANCE, BELGIUM:
Interart Paris, www.interart.fr

UK:
Central Books Ltd, www.centralbooks.com

USA, CANADA, CENTRAL AND SOUTH AMERICA, AFRICA:
ARTBOOK | D.A.P., www.artbook.com

JAPAN:
twelvebooks, www.twelvebooks.com SOUTH KOREA:
The Book Society, www.thebooksociety.org

AUSTRALIA, NEW ZEALAND:
Perimeter Distribution, www.perimeterdistribution.com

First edition   ISBN
Printed in Germany   978-3-95905-521-5